The Signature Series

_037_ of 100

Praise for *The Light Here Changes Everything*

Patrick Stockwell's *The Light Here Changes Everything* is the mesmerizing story of Sophie's against-her-will attempt to throw open the blinds on her life. An in-recovery alcoholic, Sophie finds that after reaching one year of sobriety, the most important relationships in her life—with her hard-nosed AA sponsor, her problematic boyfriend, her dead father, and her sober and un-sober selves—flicker with shadows that are darker and deeper than she suspected. This is a powerful and emotionally layered debut from a writer with tremendous talent, patience, and grace.

Joseph Scapellato, author of *The Made-Up Man* and
Big Lonesome

Every good story is a coming-of-age story; Patrick Stockwell's *The Light Here Changes Everything* is no exception. Adulthood means abadoning certain romantic notions, and Sophie's entrenchment in a kind of Western wild glamor—replete with bar brawls, road trips, guns and booze—shifts in the course of this utterly engaging novella. This character is funny and flawed and working hard at redemption in the lustrous harsh light of the real, rather than nostalgic, American west.

Antonya Nelson, author of *Funny Once* and *Bound*

Patrick Stockwell is a writer who knows how to tell a story. In *The Light Here Changes Everything*, he explores the powerful influence of personal relationships alongside the seductive dread of addiction. This is a story about trespass, about those who trespass against us, and how readily we trespass against ourselves. Stockwell's writing is crisp, infused by a satisfying forward momentum, and punctuated by moments of elevated light.

Kurt Caswell, author of *Laika's Window:*
The Legacy of a Soviet Space Dog

Gorgeous, patient and electric. This is the kind of work that restructures the reader at the atomic level. Sophie finds herself on someone else's daffy pilgrimage but damn it if she doesn't find what she didn't know she was looking for. Reminds you that self-destruction is the bastard cousin of self-creation.

David MacLean, author of *The Answer to the Riddle is Me*

The Light
Here
Changes
Everything

PATRICK STOCKWELL

Texas Review Press • Huntsville

A NOVELLA

The Light
Here
Changes
Everything

For Lee K. Abbott

Contents

Ceremony

From day one, Sophie's sponsor said to call her Adelaide, but the woman was prematurely gray at forty-six, dark-spotted and crinkle-skinned from years in the sun like a farmhouse grandmother, so people at the meetings tended to refer to her as Ms. A. It had been fifteen years since her one and only relapse—a vodka-inspired meltdown that started at her youngest child's birthday party and ended with her wrists handcuffed to a bed in the ER at Ben Taub Hospital—and the fact that a person's dignity might survive such a thing was what convinced Sophie to approach Ms. A about sponsorship. In the twelve months that followed, they hadn't gone longer than a night of broken sleep without talking.

Along with Mr. Sattler, the church activities coordinator and a fellow former drunk, Ms. A was the one who showed up first to St. Paul's Methodist ahead of Tuesday night meetings. Everyone claimed the coffee tasted better when she made it, and at least once a month she brought in enough Shipley's donuts for everyone to have at least two.

Sophie was halfway through probation after a second DUI, and Ms. A was pleased that she was completing the twelfth step by sharing her message with others. But what had dominated their conversations leading up to her one-year chip ceremony was the cross-country road trip that Sophie's boyfriend, Sid, had planned to celebrate the achievement. It was Ms. A's experience that anniversaries—first anniversaries in particular—were prime occasions for relapse. In the last group meeting, she'd led with a conversation about the "pink cloud" that tended to consume the newly sober and how hard it is to maintain abstinence once the euphoria had dissipated. Sophie had yet to feel euphoric, but it didn't stop the group from insisting that she should remain vigilant.

Ms. A picked her up before the meeting and took her for a pancake dinner. After three cups of coffee and a piece of chocolate pie, they drove to St. Paul's. The doors were still locked so they sat in the car in the air conditioning.

"It's not the camping part I'm worried about. It's the stops along the way. Las Cruces. Flagstaff. I looked them up. College towns. Desert towns." She leaned toward Sophie and let her have it with the know-it-all-mom look she used when making a particularly important observation. "Drinking towns. Not much else to do at night but go out."

Sophie thunked her head against the warm glass. "We'll be too tired for all that."

"Is he still not drinking?"

"Who knows?" She made a show of digging in her backpack, buying time until she found some words that made enough sense to say out loud. "He's been complaining, but it's not like he's in the program so I get it."

Ms. A lit two cigarettes and handed one to Sophie. She didn't crack her window. "If what you keep saying is true, he probably should be."

"I asked him to come tonight, but no one could cover the door at the Hawthorne, and he didn't want to play the 'I'm the owner's boyfriend' card."

"Have you thought any more about selling the place?"

"If I did, I think my daddy would probably come back to life just so he could die of a broken heart."

"You should at least get someone else to do your buying."

"I keep telling you that I place the orders from home. The bartenders do the stocking. I haven't gone into the building since I rehired Sid and had to train him on the new system."

Ms. A sighed hard, like it hurt her lungs to do so. "I'm worried that you're one freakout away from a binge. When you get back, I want to work on these choices. The bar. That man. Neither of them serves you."

Sophie rolled down her window and hung her head out into the wet evening heat to escape the smoke. "I'm supposed to drive us to the first stop, past the Hill Country, so he can take us the rest of the way to New Mexico."

"With a suspended license."

Sophie watched the tip of her cigarette, blowing hard to make the cherry glow brighter. "These Camels are gross."

"Stop deflecting."

"It's easier than sitting through the two-hour conversation we'll have to have about it."

Another car pulled up alongside, and Mr. Sattler shouted apologies at them as he scurried to open the building. Ms. A dropped her cigarette into an empty can of coconut water. "What's the final destination?"

"All I know is it's somewhere in the desert near Las Vegas."

"I'll keep my ringer on this week when I go to bed." Ms. A switched off the ignition and opened her door. Hot air flooded the car. "You have your speech?"

Sophie patted her pocket.

"Better lay off the coffee for the rest of the night. You've got a long road ahead of you."

The room where they had their meetings reminded her of high school, of wine coolers during off-campus lunch and being buzzed during homeroom. Crooked lines of chairs faced a podium and a banner that displayed the twelve steps in case anyone forgot. The walls were painted a glossy beige and decorated with inspirational posters thoughtfully arranged so that no matter where the eye might wander, it would land on a flash of wisdom. The quotes were unanimously taken from Tony Robbins. Once she found out that a speech could not be avoided, Sophie had been trying to find a favorite to include in her remarks. She was waffling between "If you do what you've always done, you'll get what you've always gotten" and "The past does not equal the future."

In this particular chapter, chips were presented at the end of the hour in order to guarantee that everyone left the meeting on a high note. A pair of military men were leading, veterans of respective jungle and desert wars, so most of the conversation was coded in combat metaphors. The oldest—one of the last ones home from Vietnam—concluded his remarks with the story of a recent trip to Washington, D.C., and the confusion that comes when one no longer recognizes the country they fought for.

"Standing in front of that big White House, knowing that the bastard who lives there these days don't give a squirt of goose shit for what I been through, I tell y'all right now this was the closest I come to drinking since my mama passed on a couple years back. But I thank Jesus that I had this soldier's number to call," he said, and clasped the younger man's hand. Together, they raised them overhead. "And that he had the mercy within him to answer. Wasn't even born when I was over there fighting, but we's still brothers in this battle to stay clean."

Most people stood up for this one. Still seated, Sophie enjoyed the brief anonymity that the wall of humans provided. In spite of frequent, gentle insistence from Ms. A and the other old-timers, she hadn't shared her story since the first month.

When everyone sat down again, Ms. A had her meeting face on, all smiles and wrinkled with wisdom. As she went through the list of her sponsee's achievements as a sober person, it was all Sophie could do to stay in her chair until her name was called. People turned and smiled whenever something they could relate to came up. There was a pressure in this particular kinship. It was part of what kept her from slipping, but it also made her sobriety feel that it wasn't really hers, as if she were doing it for everyone else. Like married couples staying miserable for the sake of their kids. Most days, the decision not to drink was made for her through these affirmations, and as she sat there she wondered if the choice would feel genuine once the court order had expired.

Ms. A wrapped up her remarks with her belief that "One day, sooner than she realizes, I just know that it's going to be Sophie up here telling you how proud she is of the person she's introducing." She extended a hand, beckoning. "Make some noise, friends. Make her feel how thankful we are that she's with us."

As Sophie made her way to the front of the room, the whoops and cheers and clapping weren't all that different from what she was used to hearing at the Hawthorne when she outdrank men twice her size. If competition drinking had been a sport, she'd have been a champion. The taste of tequila flooded her mouth. Ms. A put the one year chip in her hand and held her close as the applause swelled.

She set the bronze medallion in the center of the podium and traced the 'I' with her thumb. It was the one Ms. A received the first time she made a year, shiny from being held through times of crisis. The patina reminded Sophie of a statue she'd seen in pictures—Mary holding Jesus after he was dead.

If you're gonna haul ass, she told herself, you better do it now before you lose your shit in front of a room full of professional drunks.

Instead, she forced a smile and told them all "thank you" over and over until the room was finally quiet. While Sophie fidgeted with her chip, searching for the courage Ms. A claimed lay within her, this silence stretched past the point of comfort. Throats cleared. Chair legs scraped the floor. Whispers began at the back of the room and worked their way forward. Sophie wiped beads of moisture from her eyes. She slid her speech from her pocket, a page and a half of hand-written bullet points—an incomplete sum of her accomplishments—that she and Ms. A had compiled throughout the week. Now, none of it seemed worth mentioning.

If being sober was still a challenge for someone who'd fired machine guns at strangers and watched them die, she thought, how in the bloody fuck could she expect to keep herself in check when Sid went on another shopping binge and the rent check bounced again?

She turned to Ms. A, whose lips were twisting like she was holding back a shout. When she noticed Sophie's wet cheeks, she slipped into her sweet-loving-mom face and took her hand. "I think you should throw the speech away and just talk. They'll be happy with whatever you have to say."

The podium was as unstable as her concentration. Looking out across so many faces, she felt like she was back in high school, about to give a speech to the class about global warming. People sat in the same cliques as children: the athletic, the most successful, the self-marginalized. There, the difference was that the majority of those in the room were committed to the appearance that everyone was getting along.

"My name is Sophie, and I'm an alcoholic."

Everyone chimed, "Hi, Sophie."

"I don't have a whole lot to say. I owe everyone here a bunch of 'thank yous.' I owe Ms. A a whole lot more for putting up with me. Everyone I've ever seen do this has sounded like they have all their shit piled in one place. Maybe it's just me, but I can't remember a time when things felt right. Honestly, I'm not sure I feel that way now." She lit a cigarette, took a long drag, and held the lighter to the corner of her speech. "I know we're not supposed to smoke in here but this is the sort of thing I used to need a drink for, so, you'll have to forgive me."

Sophie held the burning paper till its glowing edges turned her finger-tips a deep red. She dropped it to the floor and stamped out the remaining flames. From their place in front, the two soldiers stood and clapped. Before long, the whole room was standing and a few members were lighting cigarettes of their own. Despite some shouting and arm waving from Mr. Sattler, within seconds a blanket of gray smoke floated overhead.

She turned to face Ms. A sitting in the front row. "What I can say is that I've survived. In spite of my business and the man I live with and being close to more bottles than I can count on a daily basis, I got through. Hardest of all was surviving myself—the blackouts, the trips to jail, all the legal shit. It seemed like fun. I was interesting. I had stories I could tell and plenty of people who liked hearing them." She held up the medallion and crushed out her cigarette at its center. "All week long I've been looking for words that can explain where I'm at now, and the only thing I can say with any sliver of genuine truth is that I learned how to be grateful for one hell of a boring year."

After a few closing remarks from the younger soldier, people stood together talking while Mr. Sattler made an angry show of sweeping butts. It was clear that he wanted nothing to do with Sophie, which gave her a real reason not to stay to help clean up like she usually did. She told Ms. A she was going to the bathroom and instead went straight to the car. The humidity was on full blast, and the sweat gathering at her armpits and along her spine made her regret forgoing her usual uniform of all black for a vintage polyester shirt she'd dug from the back of the closet in the hope that bright polka-dots might make her feel more festive and less of a fake, to feel she actually belonged in recovery. Instead, it felt as heavy as a wool sweater and reminded her of winter nights, sitting alone outside with no coat after closing the Hawthorne, sipping red wine to offset the damp chill, finishing a second bottle and marking it out of inventory as damaged.

She was on the verge of ripping the clothes off her body when a clump of members emerged from the building, waving and thanking her as they passed for sharing, praising her for her courage and the unorthodox delivery. A young woman, not much more than a girl and new to the group, stopped to give her a hug and gush about the night. She'd recently asked Sophie to be her sponsor before she'd known the rules that dictated whom she should ask. Ideally, the person would have every last bit of their shit together, be at least ten years sober and done with all twelve steps. Besides these, there were a few other requirements that Sophie might never possess and had therefore chosen not to remember.

"I fucking loved how you just got up there and did your thing and said 'fuck it' to everyone's expectations." The woman's hand lingered on Sophie's forearms, dark eyes wide and brimming with inflated, post-adolescent admiration. "You literally lit the place on fire. So dope."

Sophie had forgotten her name already. Beneath a swirl of hot, guilty feeling, she found a way to say "thank you" and "I'd been dreading it for weeks."

"Can we get coffee sometime? I found a sponsor at my other meeting, but he says that I should also make friends that are closer to my age." Sophie wiped the moisture from her forehead. "I'm older than you think I am."

"Well, he's like sixty-something," the woman said, smiling like Sophie had already agreed to friendship. "I haven't found a group with kids who just drink. They all did, like, H or coke or pills. When they share, they still talk about fucking strangers and getting high."

In the pause that followed, Sophie let her mind run out into a world she'd only escaped through consequence and legal supervision. Drugs had never worried her, but she could never own up to how much she missed the freedom of blackout drinking and waking up in places that held no expectations. Sid had come into her life at the beginning of a yearlong binge and, in the months that followed, through balanced and thoughtful supervision he'd discovered a way to remain. Images of his soft eyes and hard mouth clouded her view of the young woman's face, and Sophie imagined she could smell the boozy sweat beneath his deodorant, like he'd come up behind them so he might eavesdrop and become afraid.

She crushed her cigarette. "My boyfriend and I are going out of town for a couple of weeks."

"Right." The woman's face fell as she pulled her keys from her bag. "Maybe I'll see you when you get back."

Now that the night was over, Sophie's thoughts were consumed with the long drive west and plans for hotel- and desert-hopping. Sid's endless need for external validation and the temptations that came when she found herself unable to provide the words that he'd demand. The bottles of clear liquor that she'd seen him hide in the back of the Subaru behind the first aid kit and beneath the extra pillows.

It wasn't that she blamed him for her drinking but, before she got herself in trouble, liquor had become the linchpin that helped her keep it together through every hours-long conversation they'd had about going on a couple's diet, whose friends were better, or whether or not they should switch internet providers.

Ms. A had been pushing for Sophie to start looking past Sid in a not so subtle, "do what I'm suggesting or face the consequences," sort of way.

"You'd be on your own for the first time. Just you. The new you. Sober," she'd say, usually after a second or third cup of coffee, after they'd talked through the latest crisis she'd created. "I think you'll find that life or independence or just getting out of bed sometimes will seem more appealing when you're facing it on your own terms."

The Sophie that always stayed put had run this idea past her better inside-self so many times that she would sometimes say it aloud, sometimes in public, ignoring of the stares of those who found themselves in proximity to the mumblings of a recently reformed drunk.

"You've given me a lot to think about," she might say. Or, "If I try leave him before I'm really ready, he'll just talk me out of it with flowers and a *tres leches* cake."

Ms. A would shake her head like always and remind them both that she wasn't a relationship counselor by trade.

Loud voices broke the quiet as Ms. A and the two veterans emerged from the building. The men walked away in different directions down Main Street.

"Thought those boys would never stop talking," Ms. A said, pausing to stretch her legs and back. "I wish you'd been there to rescue me."

"I wouldn't know what to say to them."

"You wouldn't have to say much. Once you got going about your appreciation of all things normal, I think half the people in there'd be willing to marry you before a second date."

"Already planning for life after Sid."

"If you'll take it upon yourself to get rid of that which holds you in this ridiculous, wheel-spinning situation, you'll probably find yourself with more options than a homecoming queen."

At the thought of leaving Sid to date one of her fellow basket cases, Sophie's gut turned sour. "Is this about being sober or about finding a better relationship?"

Ms. A got into the car and opened the sunroof. "It's about living, Sophie. Why the hell did we quit drinking if we're so afraid of change?"

Whenever Ms. A hit her in the face with a line of loaded advice, Sophie felt that the woman really did want to be more of a mom than the person to call when the darkness wouldn't break.

She climbed into the passenger seat, lit a cigarette for herself and one for her sponsor, and rolled down the window. "Definitely keep your ringer on. Turn it up all the way. I've got a feeling this trip is going to help me figure out what's what."

"In the meantime, I'm going to have to figure out how to get Sattler to come back down to earth. He's in orbit over the smoke and scorched floor tiles. You could have given me the head's up about the fireworks."

"You always say I'm not a planner and that I shouldn't try to be one."

The car's headlights swept the lower limbs of an awning of live oak trees that covered Montrose Boulevard. The radio was tuned to NPR, a story about climate change and Big Agriculture. When Ms. A began to argue with the host like he was sitting in the seat behind them, Sophie shut her ears and prayed for sleep.

Sid was snoring on the living room floor with his head against an over-stuffed duffel when she got home. He was already dressed for the road, with a freshly trimmed beard. On his chest was a pad of paper, and she could see that he'd crossed off everything on his packing list.

What a fucking Boy Scout, she thought, and kissed his forehead, holding her breath in the event that his skin might stink of booze. "You still got some cuteness left in you."

She still had her own bags to pack. Looking around the apartment, she was reminded of the dorm room she'd shared with a redneck girl called Dolores Jean from Wichita Falls throughout the only year she'd been in school. Clothes hung from the furniture, sink piled with a week of dishes, carpet dotted with suspicious stains like islands on a map made of Berber. Sid's vintage gig poster collection covered most of every wall—wild, Technicolor rectangles featuring bare-chested men and women and demons with stars for eyes—but it didn't seem as edgy and offbeat as it was when he'd first moved in. The shelves of vinyl records he hoarded had limited the pieces of useful furniture to a loveseat and coffee table. The flat-screen television sat on the mantle of a fireplace that had never been used. Sophie's possessions were confined to the kitchen and a walk-in closet.

This is more of a crash pad than a place where grown people live, she thought. You're thirty-four going on nineteen, Sophie, and Sid might be seventeen. At best.

She stepped outside to smoke one more before bed. The night air had finally cooled. Insects danced against the porch light. In the near distance, a pair of cats yowled; fucking or fighting, she couldn't tell.

Ms. A was close to uncovering the truth about the reasons for keeping Sid. Drunk Sophie loved to be drunk with him, to laugh naked on the kitchen floor, to feed each other leftovers that were on the verge of turning just to offset the hangover. But it had been months since Sober Sophie had known that sort of affection, and she'd compartmentalized him into a useful hybrid of servant and sidekick. At work he played the right hand, and at home he controlled the TV remote.

She wondered if she'd really have to wait ten years to be a sponsor. Without being aware of it, Ms. A had made the job seem so appealing, like it was the only thing keeping the insane person inside her from swallowing her demons whole.

The Place to Go When
All Other Doors Were Shut

Sophie drove the first leg as planned. Per a longstanding arrangement, it was the role of the driver to stay focused on the road and the passenger's responsibility to keep them entertained and awake. Sid was in neither the condition nor the mood to do his job. He fiddled with the music, never letting one song play all the way through before he was bored and skipping ahead.

At their first stop along the interstate, a lonely gas station in Junction, Texas, Sid returned to the car with a Snickers ice cream bar, a Mexican coke, and the news that he was on the verge of a migraine and afraid to take the driver's seat.

Migraines were code for wicked hangovers, a "condition" he'd developed as a response to her sobriety.

"I've got blind spots in my peripheral vision. If it gets better, I'll take over for you when we stop in Fort Stockton."

Sophie nodded and went quickly inside to avoid having to explain why she didn't put up more of a fight. She bought energy drinks and sour candy and two packs of Marlboro lights, lingering at the counter to hear about the historically low water levels of the Llano River from the mustached clerk who seemed determined she should stick around.

"You're one of the first in a good while that wanted to know more about our little town. I try to tell everybody that comes through about the state park. Good hunting. And fishing, too, when the river's high up." The man produced a comb from his breast pocket to groom his upper lip. The tag on his blue polo shirt said his name was Ernie. "Your husband's got a temper on him. Hope I didn't cause nothing for you by talking over-long."

Sophie laughed at the man's candor. "He's not my husband. He's just a drunk."

Ernie's round face darkened with what must've been judgment—or real concern—she couldn't tell. "Well, have yourself a safe trip. I reckon you ought not to let him spoil the good parts." He held onto the bag when she tried to take from his hand. "Might not let him drive y'all neither."

Back at the car, she rolled down all four windows, cracked open the sunroof and a fresh pack of cigarettes. When Sid reminded her that he didn't want the new car to smell like smoke, she offered him the keys, which he declined.

Driving through West El Paso, Sophie nearly caused an accident by looking left through the darkness for a peek at the lights of Juárez that winked from otherwise unseen mountainsides. Sid dozed in the passenger seat and didn't stir when she jerked the wheel to avoid smashing through a row of orange construction barrels and into a crew of workers.

Near the New Mexico border, the driver of an eighteen-wheeler blasted her with a long, loud pull at the horn when she veered back into his lane.

Sid jumped, fully awake and cursing at her for not being more careful. "If I'd have known you were going play Speed Racer with a goddamned big rig, I would've taken over for you back in Fort Stockton."

"The highway's so crooked and winding, it's like driving a go-kart," She reached over and tapped at his temple. "How's your migraine?"

He sounded like a pouty ten-year-old when he said, "I just want to be out of this car."

Signs for Anthony, Vado, and Mesquite flew by. Past a scattering of porch lights, more mountains loomed in the darkness. A misguided coyote hovered near the exit for Las Cruces and darted back into the shadows when Sid launched a throaty howl through the open window.

"They've got legit wildlife out here, Soph," he said, suddenly full of life. "I read about these antelope they brought over from Africa. Big as saddle horses. They're invasive now. Ziegen Bocks, or bucks, or something. You can even shoot them without a license."

"I didn't realize this was a hunting trip."

He laughed. "If I had a rifle, maybe."

Back when she was still drinking every night, he'd signed them up for concealed carry classes. They both graduated, in spite of being drunk or high during every lesson. He hadn't left the house without a pistol since.

"You pack the Glock?"

"It's in the back. But that wouldn't do much more damage than a pellet gun. Besides, what the hell would I do with all that meat?"

Along the access road, hotel signs towered over those that advertised gas stations and strip malls. People wandered into traffic or down broken sidewalks, without purpose, oblivious to each other and oncoming traffic like characters in an art house film about the end of the world. Sophie was sure she had seen this movie but couldn't place the name. Like everything else that happened when she was drinking, the details of the experience were filed in some dark corner of her brain she'd likely never have access to again.

"This shit is totally existential, Soph." Sid was hanging out the window like a giant, happy beagle. "Can't wait to see what the locals do for fun."

Sophie was not impressed with their options. "I hope there's more to do here than hang out behind a dumpster with a forty and a pack of Black & Milds."

Their room at the back of the La Quinta faced a giant convenience store that sold burritos, made to order. Sid handed her a bean and cheese, set two more on the nightstand with some napkins, plasticware, and bottled water.

"It's already cooling down outside." His face was flushed, eyes as big around as golf balls and misty at the corners. "Cool enough to think about moving here. Get away from the bugs and swampy air back home."

Sophie stared at him until he recognized that if he wanted her with him he shouldn't entertain that thought for more than a minute.

"We made it." He held up his water for a toast. "To us."

Sophie had finished half the bottle before she realized he wanted her to reciprocate. "To—" she began and lost the thought for fear that its sentiment might fail the moment he seemed to require. Her eyes searched the desert-pink walls for inspiration before landing on a painting of several cracked clay pots. "To putting ourselves back together."

They drained their bottles and refilled them from the sink. Sid had his thinking face on, lips folded inside his mouth, eyebrows pushed together. Clearly, he'd found something to be disappointed with. She chewed through a bite of greasy cheese and bean paste, waiting for a complaint that never came.

Instead, he asked her what sort of night she felt like having. "Let's go somewhere. It's barely nine o'clock, and Flagstaff is close enough that we don't have to worry about what time we hit the road." His smile was genuine, loose and toothy, more like those she remembered from their earliest days together than the straight-lined grimace she'd come to expect. "The needle on my give-a-fuck meter just hit one hundred percent."

Sophie could feel the burrito sitting heavy in her gut, and she imagined that it had returned to its original, uneaten shape. In the past, whenever Sid talked about his give-a-fuck meter, it often meant he was committed to one of two things: saving their relationship or getting blackout drunk. She'd never seen him passionate about anything else and, without context, she could only speculate as to which direction his urges would take them.

"It's not like I spent a week on the Internet searching for 'things to do in Las Cruces,'" she said as she pulled off her clothes to take a shower. "Figured you had the whole itinerary nailed down anyway."

His eyes never left her face. "I was thinking we might order a ride and see what the driver recommends."

He nodded when she asked if he was wearing the clothes he had on, a short-sleeved camping shirt from the outdoor store, fratty cargo shorts, and the worn out old man sandals he'd owned since before she met him. Sophie pulled clothes from her suitcase, tops and bottoms in varying shades of black, holding them up to herself in the mirror until she settled on the right combination of a tank top and jeans.

"You know this is a desert trip, Sophie? Black's better for funerals and vampires."

As she closed the bathroom door, she caught his reflection in the mirror. He was staring at her backside, pupils dilated. They hadn't shared more than a hug and a quick peck in weeks and, since she'd sobered up, they'd only slept in bed together a couple of nights a week. If she felt like sex at all, it was short and to the point. The hunger he'd been swallowing never showed unless he thought she wasn't looking, sneaky looks when she was changing into her pajamas or, like now, when she was walking the other way.

Try as she might, the water in the shower was either too hot or too cold and smelled like sulfur.

His hopeful enthusiasm, though fraught with accumulated anxiety, was knocking against the brick wall she'd made to guard her sobriety. Her skin warmed against the chill of the water, and when she was getting dressed, she left her clean underwear on the bathroom floor and traded her jeans for a skirt. Lying on the carpet with his face six inches from the road atlas, Sid didn't notice her until she put her bare foot on the page bearing the map of Arizona. His eyes slid up her leg and settled past her hemline. In another minute, he was singing in the shower. Sophie picked a clean outfit for him, wrinkled but clean cargo pants and a short-sleeved collared shirt in plaid, and laid it on the bed.

She called her Ms. A, who picked up on the first ring. "You kill him yet?"

Why lie? she thought. "I decided to try a different approach."

"If you call me later tonight to tell me you slipped, I might have to drive to—where are you exactly—and drag your ass to a 9 A.M. meeting."

Sophie heard a match strike and a long exhale. Ms. A smoked tobacco the way a stoner smokes a joint. Pull it in deep and hold on as long as you can so your lungs can absorb every precious molecule of the good stuff. Cigarettes weren't as kind to the body, but after three decades of this more pleasant self-abuse, she was too dug in to the habit to escape from it.

"I'm in southern New Mexico. Forty something miles past the state line. About the same distance down to the border." Standing before the mirror, Sophie ran a hand across the front of her skirt and tugged it down to a length that looked presentable. "I think I just decided that I'm going to try fucking him."

In the middle of a drag, Ms. A choked and started hacking. The only word she could muster was "Why?"

"I was talking to this weird little man at a gas station who suggested that I shouldn't let 'my husband' spoil the trip for me."

"That should tell you something, Sophie. If a stranger in the middle of nowhere can tell that Sid is the one dark cloud in a blue sky—"

"You're verging."

"On what?"

"On making my decisions for me before you get the whole story. Before I've had a chance to decide if I can make them on my own."

Ms. A let that hang while she muttered to herself. "Is this one of your famous whims or something you've seriously considered?"

"Does it matter?"

"Right. Like when you were thinking about fooling around with that chiropractor, the one with the giant hands." Ms. A started laughing, which segued into wheezy coughing. Eventually, she pulled it together. "Seemed like a good time to replay old conversations."

They talked for a while about strategy. In the end, Ms. A was forced to admit that using sex as a peacekeeping mechanism was preferable to pretending that he wasn't an annoying man-child for ten days. "I hope your birth control prescription is up to date."

"It is. But I haven't shaved anything in months."

"It's been quite a while for you two and, if my memory serves me, I don't think it would take him more than a couple of minutes anyway."

However honest it might be, Ms. A's suggestion robbed any hope of pleasure Sophie thought to have from the moment when it came around. Drinking was often necessary to make it fun—or more bearable. There were bottles hidden in the back of the Subaru, tucked behind the first aid kit and beneath the extra pillows. The keys were on the desk to her right. Another silence. Another match lighting.

She was pissed at how easily the thought of alcohol took over—cheap vodka specifically—and how a sudden flood of saliva held a specific proximity to rubbing alcohol. Worse, if even Ms. A and her stone-cold lock on sanity could trigger it, Sophie wondered how easy would it be for some random thought to shut down her own fragile will.

It was Ms. A that finally broke the quiet. "Is he still in the shower or are you talking about all of this with him sitting there in front of you?"

"No, he just started singing another song."

"Don't know about you, but pruny skin on a man hits me right in the bikini area."

The conversation derailed when a shirtless Sid poked his head through the door to say he'd requested their ride. He looked at his phone. "You got about seven minutes. Tell Ms. A I said 'hello.'"

The driver's name was William. Contemporary Christian music played quietly on satellite radio. The car smelled like artificial cherry air freshener with a hint of fresh coffee wafting from the lidless cup in his hand. Within the first three minutes of the ride he had shared with them that he was a retired Marine sergeant, still married after twenty-nine years, the father of two sons who attended the local university. He was born in the neighboring town of Mesilla and had come back with his family after some time spent abroad during three "desert tours."

In the back seat, Sophie moved closer to Sid and put a hand on his leg, hoping to distract him from his conversation with the driver. But he was still in a good mood and full of questions. He had yet to settle on a destination. "Why do you think people come back here?"

Try as he might, William seemed to be having a hard time explaining what it was he liked about the town. "Anyone with a pair of decent glasses can see that the place isn't exactly overflowing with money. Rent's cheap. The beer's expensive. The mountains are nice for hiking if that's what you're into. Most people stay home to entertain so except for the cops and a few night owls like me it's a ghost town after ten o'clock."

Sophie caught William's eyes in the mirror. He lifted his chin and smiled. "Hate to change the subject, but I think the lady wants to know where it is I'm taking you."

"Where do the rest of the night owls gather?"

"There's a couple of sports bars back toward campus. You can get burger and hear some music, though I'm told the bands are never very good."

"Sophie doesn't drink."

"Good for Sophie." William's reflection smiled at her again, but he had yet to address her directly. He looked to Sid. "I gave it up myself when my first son was born."

Whether it was being talked about or what was being said, she couldn't tell, but she was ready to be done with the ride. She wished she'd put the underwear in her bag. She wished she could start yelling until they decided where to go.

"So where do people go to hear the good music?" Sid asked, moving Sophie's hand and leaning forward.

"I drive a lot of people out to this place in the old neighborhood, Old Mesilla. Me and my buddies used to go there back before I enlisted. Before I was old enough to understand that whiskey was not my friend." He typed the address into his phone to log the fare. "The place has quite a history. I'll run you over so you can stick your head in to see if it's the sort of fun you're in need of."

Sophie's mouth turned sticky with thirsty memories that she wanted to spit out onto the floorboard. "Is there anything there for me to drink?"

When William didn't respond right away, Sid answered for him. "We'll get club sodas with lime in tall glasses and long straws. Pretend we're drinking like fancy people."

The car turned down a long road, a tree-lined tunnel through the darkness with few streetlights to mark the way. At the end of this road stood a collection of pale, blocky buildings that might have been condemned if they belonged to a larger city. William made confusing turns down narrow streets, dodging through a more appealing set of pedestrians and vehicles, like they'd crossed an invisible barrier between the land of apathy and a place where the business of living still mattered. Sophie got dizzy looking out the window at so much activity in such a confined space. Her stomach did a flip-flop.

Along the town square, William slowed to a stop in front of a low adobe building surrounded by various assortments of smokers. Sid jumped out of the car and closed the door in her face before he realized she was trying to follow him. Now that they were alone, William's eyes were on her in the mirror. She set her jaw and held the stare as he sipped his coffee.

Sid came to the door on her side. "This is the place."

Sophie nearly fell getting out of the back seat. She moved to join a small group of women smoking to one side of the bar. College girls of legal age talking about their boyfriends and the men they wish they were dating instead. She lit a cigarette, bummed one to a young woman who asked, and stepped away for a moment to get her head situated with what was about to go down.

Back home, this bar would have been an afterthought, a last resort, a place on the fringe of the city that you went to when you were trying to save money or be openly affectionate with a secret lover without being seen. In this strange desert city, it was something special. Timeless. Historic. The place to go when all other doors were shut. Every square inch of the joint was in need of a facelift. The cowboy art and beer signs, faded newspaper clippings in crooked frames, the pool table—stained with dark shapes resembling islands—that sloped visibly to one side. Even the band was tired, older men in Hawaiian shirts playing wobbly covers of songs written by other men who would have been old when they were still young. The number of hands that clapped at the end of their set could be counted with less than ten fingers.

With a playlist built by younger drinkers, the digital jukebox screamed to life. Hip-hop mixed with New Country, weekend songs about screwing and drinking and getting high. Sophie stood against the back wall, watching Sid become irritated behind a wall of townies and college bros stacked three deep at the bar. They'd been inside for half an hour.

A tall man in a black leather blazer—shoulders wider than a doorframe—paused on his way to the bathroom and touched her shoulder. "You look like you could use a drink or two and a decent fellow to buy them for you."

She moved her bag between them and crossed her arms. "I've got both those things covered, but thank you." She looked toward the bar for Sid, who had disappeared. "My boyfriend will be back any minute."

"I didn't ask if I could feel your ass, now did I?" A flicker of aggression lit behind his glassy eyes. He was carrying three times her weight and looked like he could take a bullet to the chest and still keep drinking. "Everybody's family in here. We don't mind strangers, but strangers that stand in the corner looking like they just got a whiff of road kill might want to move on out. You must be some sort of special I've never heard of."

"No, sir, I just—"

"You just nothing." He put his large hand in front of her face.

She moved down the wall to stand behind a group of twenty-some-things in flannel and dark denim who looked as out of place as she felt. They were complaining about the band, the crowd, and that the drinks were more expensive than the dives they'd been to before. The young woman who'd bummed a cigarette from her earlier was with them.

When Sophie caught her eye, she smiled and came to stand beside her. "You here alone?"

"Feels like it." Sophie pointed toward the bar. "The guy I'm with is over that way."

"It's busy for a Wednesday. The band sucks, but I guess they brought in some people. Usually it's just us and some regulars that come in when they get off from their restaurant jobs."

Her new friend's name was Bonnie. She and her friends were from the university, graduate students trying to get some hard drinking done before the new semester began.

Bonnie fished an olive from her dirty martini and offered it to Sophie. She took it without thinking and nearly popped it in her mouth. The woman looked past her when someone from her group called out, and Sophie dropped the olive in her bag and pretended to swallow when she turned back.

They talked about the city and its limited options for fun. Bonnie was from Denver. She was used to options. "Sometimes I'm sorry that I passed on Colorado State to come here. We all think about transferring, but none of us ever do it."

The band was back onstage, tuning guitars and tapping drumheads. Garth Brooks came on the jukebox, and suddenly most everyone was singing about their friends in low places. The bass player started playing along, slightly offbeat, and the effect made Sophie dizzy.

Bonnie put her glass in Sophie's hand. "Drink the rest of this. Your boy-friend's taking forever, and I need another cigarette."

The woman left with some of her friends in tow. The only empty table was just behind the giant man, now back from the bathroom, sitting with two other giant men. They looked like a hit squad. Sophie stared at the drink in her hand, cloudy with olive juice, lipstick marks at the rim. She could smell the vinegar and, beneath it, a hint of danger. It had been almost forty-five minutes, but Sid wouldn't dream of giving up before he'd been served. If he saw her holding the martini, she wasn't sure if he'd be concerned that she was slipping or celebrate that they could drink together again.

She got her answer immediately when he appeared, finally, with a drink in each hand. A man from the bar had come with him bearing two more. They kept moving in the direction of the pool table. Sophie followed. A couple was finishing up a game. Once the last ball had dropped, they shook hands with Sid and his new companion and leaned against the wall to watch the next round. The band was slaughtering its way through "Black Magic Woman."

"This is Trevor," Sid said, feeding quarters into the table. "State law says you can only carry two at a time so he volunteered to help me out."

Trevor nodded and set them up for a game of 8-ball. Sid took the martini from her hand without asking where it came from, set it on a high table, and kissed her to the right of her lips like he did when he didn't want her to taste alcohol. Still, a whiff of lime and tequila caught her attention.

He was unapologetic. "I had to bribe him with a shot to let us play. Wouldn't take it unless I had one too."

"Just one?"

"He bought the second round while we were talking."

While you were talking, she thought.

The crowd thinned, driven away by the band and the competition for fresh drinks. Sid went back to the bar for a round of shots when Trevor, who was good enough to hustle anyone, ran the table in three turns. The couple—some friends of Trevor's from work—were too into themselves for conversation. Sophie shielded her lime and soda with her bag, caught Trevor's eye, held up a cigarette, and when he nodded she scooted carefully through clumps of people to the door.

Bonnie was alone on the smoking bench, crying to her mother in her cellphone that she'd been left behind by her friends because she wasn't ready to leave when they were. Sophie lingered close until she could see she wasn't needed and moved a few feet down the sidewalk to smoke and call Ms. A.

"I can hear the ice clinking in that glass, Soph." She cleared her throat the way she did before a lecture, before Sophie had a chance to mess things up. "How many have you had?"

"It's club soda," she said, and told her about the martini, what the smell of it did to her and how she felt more normal than she had in ages by just having it in her hand.

"So you didn't drink it." Not a question. A statement of relief.

"I'm finding that if I can just sit through the impulse until something comes along to distract me I'm good."

Ms. A put on her mom voice, the irritated version. "It's still early."

She gave Sophie a scripted pep talk. "Walk away when you feel the need to. Do your breathing. Picture my face—my ugliest, most pissed off face—when you're thinking you might pick up a drink."

Eventually, they ran out of things to say and hung up. From Sophie's perspective, there was only so much talking that could be done before it lost meaning, usefulness, and became a flat puddle of words. For the past year, she'd barely thought about anything besides drinking. Not because she wanted one. That was a recent development. More than anything, the idea of not drinking and the work that it required kept being sober foregrounded in her mind as an institution. Admitting that "I am a drinker" meant the same thing to her as saying "I'm an alcoholic." The only difference was audience, those who still practiced and those who'd learned to refrain. The only common dominator was the self and the ambiguity that came with not knowing or caring which side she was on at any given moment.

She looked for Bonnie, but the young woman had disappeared. The blunted thunder of drums and bass bled through the adobe walls of the bar. AC/DC, she thought. "You Shook Me All Night Long."

A text from Ms. A: *Going to bed but I'm here if you need me.* It was getting close to midnight.

Voices came to her from the darkness beyond the streetlights, people laughing as they wandered through down black streets, dogs barking as they passed. The night air was clear and dry. It nipped at her bare shoulders as a breeze drifted past, bringing unfamiliar desert smells. Dried grass and some sort of plant that reminded her of treated lumber. There were farm smells too—fresh cow shit most prominently. Sophie closed her eyes as band noise gave way to nightbird songs and the clicks and buzzing of insects.

The decision to remain outside came easy. Sid would come looking eventually.

"This is peace," she said out loud. "This is peace." For who knows how long, there was no other thought but this.

Men shouting from around the corner—evidently, a fight that had started inside had moved out to the street—interrupted the fragile quiet. Anxious to remain unnoticed, she moved deeper into the shadows to wait for this assault on her privacy to end.

One voice was larger than the rest, and it sounded like the speaker, or screamer, had an internalized megaphone. For the moment, the man's vocabulary was limited to obscenities that slurred together, a mess of unmitigated anger.

A body rolled to a stop in the middle of the street and remained still. She recognized the outfit, cargo pants and a plaid collared shirt. Against every protective instinct she had left, she stayed where she was. Like any casual spectator, she was dying to see what happened next.

Seconds later, the man in the leather blazer stepped into view. She wasn't surprised to learn that it was his voice she'd heard shouting. He leaned over Sid, stared quietly, and poked him in the leg as if to determine whether or not he was still breathing.

He turned to face the bar. "You think I killed the guy?"

The man's friends came to stand beside him, followed shortly by Trevor and the male half of his couple friends. One of the large men held his hand below Sid's nostrils. "Nah. I'd say he's either knocked out or damned good at playing possum."

Sophie punched in 911 on her phone and paused before placing the call. Sid was no stranger to fighting. He'd been the door guy at her favorite club when they'd first met. She trusted him to handle himself, and when he couldn't, he was pretty good at finding ways to get someone else to do it for him.

Leather blazer guy poked him again, this time with a booted toe, and turned Sid on his back. Before it went any further, Trevor stepped in between them with an offer to buy the man another drink as a peace offering. The moment the door creaked opened and slammed shut, Sid stood up and started brushing dirt from his clothes. Instead of calling for help, Sophie ordered a ride back to the hotel.

Sid peered into the shadows. "Sophie?"

She put down her empty drink and came into the light. When she was beside him, he took her cigarette from her lips and smoked the rest of it. "Thanks."

"Look at you. Making friends."

Other than a swipe of road rash along his left jaw and a tear to his shirtsleeve, he seemed intact. He shrugged. "Dude wanted the pool table before we were done with it."

"I'm guessing there's a story."

None of it was worth hearing, but he told her anyway. He was drunk. The guy was drunker. Apparently, there was a strict but unspoken three-game limit that he and Trevor had violated. When he didn't back down, the man went "volcanic."

"Said he was going to 'kick the Jesse Dogshit' out of me. Told him my dog's name was Willie Nelson." Even his laugh was slurry. "His boys thought it was funny."

She caught a blast of tequila on his breath and stepped away as a familiar car pulled up beside them. William bounced out to open the door for them. "Glad to see you folks again."

Bonnie appeared, wet-faced and shaking, begging for a ride to the other side of town. One of the bartenders had offered her a lift, but not until her shift ended at two. When Sid denied her, in spite of a small resurgence of compassion, Sophie didn't protest.

"You know that girl?" Sid said, and laid his head in Sophie's lap.

"As much as you can know any stranger that forces a drink on you."

"If I was a single fella, I might have let her tag along."

"If you were a single fella, I think she'd have asked someone else."

"Maybe she likes you." He pawed up at her face, intending to be playful, but his fingers felt like small, cold hammers. The drinks were coming on fast.

"Shut your eyes. And your mouth, while you're at it."

After a minute and a half of inebriated compliments and assurances that he loved her more than anyone, he descended into quivery sleep.

Without Sid to talk to, the driver had nothing to say. Sophie stared out the window as they drove past what looked like fields of cotton, puffs of white like tiny clouds at the side of the road. She wondered what the area looked like in daylight, if there was some beauty to be found in all this empty space. Through the windshield, the lights of Las Cruces climbed up toward the mountains, a view that aspired to be beautiful and fell short.

William turned up his Christian music, singing along with a rock band that wanted desperately to be alternative. While the lyrics spoke almost morbidly of the healing power of holy blood, the chords the band used were too fat and happy-sounding to pull off any sense of genuine angst.

This late at night, there was no one else on the road and nothing to look at but the darkened windows of businesses that were either closed for the day or closed for good. She could see the sign for their hotel in the distance. William's eyes were on her in the rearview. At some point, without her noticing, he'd tilted it down toward her chest. She held her forearm across her nipples, which were still erect from the evening chill. When he dropped them at their door, she didn't tell him thank you or leave a tip.

Sid managed to crawl to the bed on his own and was snoring before Sophie settled in. She changed into sweatpants and played on her phone for a while, buzzing through social media feeds, finding nothing but depressing arguments around the president's Twitter issues and pictures of the solar eclipse that had happened the day before.

Hard as it was to admit, she wasn't mad at him for drinking like she'd thought she'd be. In truth, in that split second she felt nothing toward him at all. It was only the first day. Sid had time to redeem himself.

What bothered her most was that she had let herself want something. To feel something more than anxiety. To begin to discover what normal looked like without the dubious safety of old habits.

"Rest well, idiot," she said, kissed her fingertips, and planted them in the center of his clammy forehead.

The dry New Mexico air had zapped the moisture from her body to leave a scratch in her throat that the hard and bitter hotel water couldn't seem to touch. She picked up her bag and walked across the street to the big convenience store. Just before one in the morning, the lights were on but the doors were locked. She tapped the glass with her keys, hoping for a response that never came. On her way back to the room, a homeless woman with a buzzcut and an overstuffed backpack asked her for a dollar. Sophie gave her what change she had and offered her a cigarette, which the woman politely declined.

She sent a text to Ms. A. *Talk?*

The Subaru was situated in a parking space in a dark spot between light poles. She opened the hatch and sat down to drink a quarter of the gallon of water. Sid had packed in case they broke down along the highway. With her legs swinging, she thought about the next day, the seven-hour drive to Flagstaff, and another night of hard work to stay focused. She'd read online that the hotel they were staying in was a landmark in the area, and the staff maintained a bar on two of its three floors and a third in the basement. The one on the top floor was six feet from the door to their room.

She sent a second text. *You up?* Sixty seconds later. *Please? Struggling.*

For every minute that passed, she sent a text, hoping that the frequency of alerts would bring Ms. A to life. After sending more than a dozen with no response, she had drained the last of her patience and begun to spiral. The cool air did nothing to relieve the heat that flushed her skin. She drank more water, but there was no way it would quench the flash fire that now consumed her.

Out of options, she called Ms. A and left a voicemail. "Hi. It's me. You said you'd be there if I needed you." She paused as if her sponsor might respond. "Anyway. I need you. He's dead asleep. Full of tequila. My plan didn't work after all." A security vehicle passed, slowing down to check her out. "It's creepy and weird here. The people have two modes: indifference or aggression." She felt beneath the extra pillows that were behind her to the right. "We were getting along for once." Her hand touched cold glass. "Anyways, I'm about to do something stupid, and I'd hoped you could talk me out of it." She was trying to discover the right goodbye when the message reached its time limit.

It was a half-pint bottle, just enough vodka to fill a rocks glass with only a splash of soda.

She had to get it out of her system, she told herself. One day at a time can always start over again tomorrow.

Cracking that seal brought her more pleasure than a hand in her pants. The clear liquid slid down her throat like honey, coating all those dried out places that the desert air had parched. Each gulp was the rough equivalent of a shot. Halfway through a second bottle, Sophie reached her limit. She'd heard that a person's tolerance remains fixed at the level it was when they stopped drinking. But in that moment, the level of buzz that was coming on was the exact right thing she'd needed. It didn't bother her in the slightest when she poured the balance on the concrete.

How long had it been since she'd been mindful? The thought occurred, the action followed. Purposeless and yet, somehow, driven.

She closed her eyes as the liquor moved inside her like a lover. Like firm, smooth hands that had memorized the places she most enjoyed being touched. Behind her knees, the points of her hips, the nape of her neck. A tingle accumulated between her legs and she let her hands follow that feeling. Above her were more stars than she had seen in years. They shifted as she watched them, and when she closed her eyes, they were still there.

When Sophie came awake again, she was sitting naked on the toilet with another bottle, empty, in her lap. Had she finished a third? The pain that ran throughout her body seemed to confirm that she had, ears ringing with cricket sounds, heart beating at her temples. Beneath this, she heard music. A ringtone. Was it Sid's?

It was hers. The screen showed that she had eight missed calls from Ms. A, all since 2 A.M. The text messages had devolved from sincere questions to a line of exclamation marks and assorted mad-faced emojis. When another call came through, she rejected it on the first ring and switched the phone to silent.

Useless Talk

They were on the road at eleven. When Sid stopped in San Antonio, New Mexico, for a "world famous green-chile cheeseburger," she'd slept in the passenger seat. He'd driven past Albuquerque before she was able to sit upright. The sun was dropping to the western horizon above Interstate 40, and it reached past her sunglasses to crank up the tension behind her eyes.

The playlist was populated with ambient music, the songs he played to collect his thoughts after they'd been fighting. She began to prepare herself to endure the near limitless philosophical tirade that usually came when the last track had ended.

But instead of being angry, he was penitent. "Did I make you do that?"

No one made her do anything, she thought. "Last night I became who I was a year ago. Then I went to bed and woke up now, a year later."

His voice was trembling as he described how scared he was when he woke up to find her lying on her side next to him with vomit around her mouth. Beside her open mouth, the pillowcase was crusty with vodka and liquefied burrito.

"If you'd been flat on your back you would've choked to death. Like those rock stars you hear about, back in the seventies." He squeezed her thigh too hard. "They all died when they were twenty-seven, almost the exact same age as you."

She tried to laugh, but it made her queasy. "You been planning for my funeral?"

A caravan of motorcycles came up behind them and roared past, moving two by two in smooth formation like a school of fish avoiding a predator. The men had beards that hung to their chests. The women had ponytails to match. All of them wore black leather vests with back patches that identified they were all a part of a "club."

Sid backed off the gas to let them pull further ahead. "I hate these fuckers."

"It was something that had been coming on for days." Sophie said as she turned to face him. "Something I had to do."

He nodded and started a new playlist. Classics from "the heyday of rock and roll." The first song was by The Doors. He turned it up and started singing. Before the second verse had ended, she asked him to turn it back down.

In Flagstaff, Sophie went to bed at seven o'clock and woke up twelve hours later. Staring at the pink walls around her, it took her a second to remember where she was. Sid had an arm across his eyes. His breathing was regular and deep. She slipped into a pair of jeans and a black sweater, unplugged her phone, and stepped out onto the third floor balcony to smoke a cigarette. The morning was bright and shockingly cold. From where she stood, she could see mountaintops and tall evergreens. Along the rooftops, large crows outnumbered the pigeons. A train whistle blew in the distance, and on the street below joggers and dog-walkers greeted each other with a friendly wave. Pedestrians stood together in conversation, hot drinks in their hands, dressed in heavy layers of flannel and wool and puffy down jackets like they were about to go for a hike or scale a rock face. The city was built for outdoor living. It seemed like everyone belonged.

After several minutes waiting for a response to her "good morning" text, she became impatient and called Ms. A's house phone. Someone picked up on the third ring, but said nothing. Sophie listened to the person breathing until she heard them light a match.

"Goddamn, this place is like a postcard," Sophie said. "Everywhere you turn there's something you haven't seen before."

This manicured silence was how Ms. A dealt with her own feelings when she was disappointed. The molten force of her anger was so direct that the phone felt hot against Sophie's ear. But it allowed her sponsor to think carefully about how to rip Sophie a new one in the nicest possible way. Usually, this nervous calm was followed by a forced recitation of the Serenity Prayer. But not today.

Ms. A sighed audibly between slurps at her coffee. It was up to Sophie to bridge the damage that came from being ignored.

This wasn't how a sponsor is supposed to handle this, she told herself. They've got your back no matter how hard you hit the ground when you fall.

It seemed best to remain neutral. "If you can't talk right now, I can try again later."

"I'm not mad at you, Sophie. If anything, I'm just out of words."

Probably for the best, she thought. "Can I share with you how it happened?"

"That's a good place to start."

Including every detail, from William's creepy eyes in the mirror to Sid's blackout performance in the street, the story took longer tell than she could have anticipated. At some point, Ms. A had stopped listening, having formed an opinion, clearly, that she was strangely reluctant to share. Every pause in the narrative was left hanging as Ms. A refused to engage with Sophie, waiting instead for the tale to end on its own.

"I'm not sure if I'm ready for what's coming," Sophie said, when she was finished. "And I'm not sure if you're giving me the silent treatment or you really have nothing to contribute."

She watched a young woman in knee-high boots clomping past the hotel. In the quiet morning air, antique hinges creaked when she opened the front door to a teashop on the bottom floor of the apartment building across the street. From this high perch, the shop looked warm and deliberately bohemian with giant pillows and deep couches and splashes of jewel tones throughout, the sort of place she'd always wanted to hang out in but never did because they seldom served alcohol.

Sid hated tea. Would hate the vibe of such a place on principle. She told herself she would get away from him for an hour to rediscover how being sober in social spaces would feel.

"You should take a hard look at where this is headed. Where you could easily wind up when you get back home. Or before."

The words leapt from Sophie's mouth before she could think to stop them. "I had to get it out of my system."

"I think you need to revisit step eleven. Do some praying. See what comes out of it."

Conversations involving a higher power had never gone well with other addicts she'd encountered, including Ms. A, who suggested that if she couldn't find a deity to rely on, she should address her cries for help "to whom it may concern."

Sophie watched as the woman at the teashop set out a sign advertising lemon scones. Music drifted through the open door, a solo piano over dreamy synthesizers. The notes hung, trembling, in the clear air. Even the crows seemed to pause their squabbles to listen. Ms. A was still talking when Sophie put the phone to her chest and closed her eyes as the music reached a crescendo, too cinematic to be believed.

Time for the subject to change. "I'm sure I told you that we're doing some exploring today. Pueblo ruins and petroglyphs." Sophie was surprised that she could still experience excitement. "There's plenty of quiet out there for me to fixate on how bad I'm fucking up."

A slurp of coffee. "Being passive aggressive about it isn't going to save you the next time you're staring at a bottle."

Sid appeared on the balcony beside her, his hair standing on end like a rooster comb, eyes pinched tightly against the bright morning light. His breath was nearly toxic when he kissed her, but she returned it anyway and squeezed his hand.

Brush your damn teeth, she mouthed through a smile. To Ms. A she said, "I'm starving. Call you later?"

Despite being an hour behind schedule, Sid's mood was lighter than she expected. They had breakfast at a nearby diner with a rowdy waitstaff and biscuits as big as a fist. Sophie felt the same nerves she might have on a first date. They sat on the same side of a booth, thighs touching. He ordered for them both, and as they carved through plates of eggs and carbohydrates, she found herself looking forward to spending time with him—genuinely—and anxious to be on the way.

The drive north to the ruins was its own adventure. A convoy of large trucks bearing Ponderosa pine logs in staggered formation took up both lanes so that Sid had to weave between them like the lead driver in a race. The soundtrack was vintage metal—Zeppelin, Black Sabbath, and early Judas Priest—all heavy drums and dark guitar buzz, an urgency that contrasted with the volume of open sky to push them toward their destination. By the time they came to the entrance for the park, Sophie's chest was so tight with anticipation she could barely inhale her cigarette.

The park road was smooth and empty. Deep green bushes dotted the dry grass of the pastureland around them. Here and there were flashes of pink and red stone and the occasional boulder thrown from a nearby volcano, dusky and porous. Finally, she realized, it felt like she was on fucking vacation. In its simplicity, its basicness, the thought was a confession. What happened in Las Cruces was left there. It was impossible to hold a negative thought in the midst of so much stony wildness. Ms. A wouldn't believe it if Sophie told her she felt disconnected from her history for the first time since they'd met.

Sid turned down a side road toward a scattering of lesser ruins. As they approached, square structures in various stages of collapse appeared along low ridgelines. They shared a cigarette, topped off water bottles and retied hiking boots, and crunched down a worn path past signs that pleaded for visitor to leave things as they found them.

"What you think, Soph?" He called to her over his shoulder. "I do okay?"

She looked past him down the path. "So far, you're okay, and getting better."

At the first small dwelling, they crawled through a square hole that served as the door, careful not to touch the walls. Flat squares of sandstone, carved or collected from the walls of the shallow box canyon that ran below, were held in place by a concrete made of sand. The ends of ancient roof beams remained visible and sponge-shaped chunks of igneous rock were thoughtfully arranged above window openings, clever choices in design that had survived the elements for more than nine centuries. Sophie watched a small black lizard climb past her, unafraid of their presence, to the top of the wall.

She took a sip of water to quench the tickle at the back of her throat. "What is it about this place that feels so different?"

"I'm not sure yet, but I'm in tune with what you're saying."

After exploring a few more small houses, they drove to the next site. Sid used his phone to take pictures of the land around them, the juxtaposition of various greens against the bluest of skies and the full spectrum of red stone, the peaks of extinct volcanoes and the San Francisco Peaks in the distance, even sneaking a few shots of her admiring the view when he thought she wasn't looking. They followed a paved walkway around a large hill to the ruin that covered it entirely. From the top, the view was staggering. All three hundred and sixty degrees of the horizon were visible, interrupted only by low mountains that didn't so much intrude on these vistas as punctuate their enormity. Except for a steady wind flowing to them across a rocky crater nearby, the world was silent and still. Conversation between them fell to hushed observations of this or that beautiful thing that should not be missed.

The structure was nearly flattened. Only a few walls remained standing. Walking across these collapsed partitions, Sophie felt like both an intruder and an invited guest. An unexcavated history slept beneath her feet, and she was afraid that her steps might rupture some long established peace.

"Do you feel like we're trespassing?" she said. "There's an energy in this one that the others didn't have. Like it's more important or something.

Like it's holy."

Sid took a seat on a patch of eroded sand that had collected near one corner and patted the spot beside him. "All I know is that for the first time in who knows how long my brain is empty. No thoughts."

For several minutes they sat alone together, watching the desert. All of Sophie's attention was given to the silence and a growing feeling of being enclosed, embraced, overtaken by the welcome nothing that had claimed her. The nagging, the all-consuming vigilance that had plagued her throughout her sobriety was for one fragile instant suppressed.

When Sid turned to her, about to speak, Sophie pressed her lips to his to preserve the sanctity of the moment. His hands cradled her face, and the kiss continued until the sound of tires on the road broke in. The driver slowed and a passenger waved to them before the RV continued on, deeper into the park. The sun erased the shadows from his face. His eyes were as hopeful as she had ever seen them. She untied his boots and pulled off his clothing, then her own, and pushed him to his back.

The sweat dried quickly as they lay beside each other, backs against the sand, naked from the waist down in the late morning sun, watching a pair crows floating on wind currents high above. Sid took one of her cigarettes, and they shared it. It was only after another car passed by that they reluctantly got dressed.

He moved to the edge of the ruins. Several other structures were visible in the distance beyond.

"They had a whole community here. This one we're standing in is like a fort. Maybe that's what's different about this place."

She stepped behind him and reached beneath his shirttail to feel the taut skin of his belly. "Whatever it is, I never want to leave."

He half-turned. "Where would we sleep?"

They were distracted by a herd of seven antelope that emerged from the shadows near the bottom of the crater, moving in loose formation toward the south. The buck stood between them and the rest of the animals, chewing and huffing occasionally, until he felt his family was far enough from danger for him to follow. Sophie shuddered and pulled back when the feeling that they were violating something sacred returned.

Sid scanned the horizon one last time and turned to go.

"One thing you can't help but notice is the light. Even back in town, it's like I can see better, shapes and colors." He turned to leave and reached out for her hand. "The light here changes everything."

Bizarre frustration gripped her chest, and she realized how badly she'd wanted to be the one to diagnose this, to give the shift in perception a name, to elevate it, claim its power, and internalize it. If and when she told friends or family the details of this journey, it was going to be difficult to give him credit.

"Don't leave me hanging, Soph." He wiggled his hand like a lure, like she might not be aware he'd offered it.

She stepped forward, arms folded. "I'm nervous to leave this place."

"Leaving is the easy part. You just get in the car and go."

Go where? she asked herself. Every destination held the promise of bad decisions, the immense risk of failing. The tingles that lingered in her belly dissipated like insects released from a jar, and she knew he would never be a part of getting them back. "Then what would you say is the hard part?"

"Remembering that you were ever here to begin with."

She took his hand and let him lead her down the path, pausing to read the information provided by the park about the first residents of the area and their community—the *Sinagua*, or "people without water"—whose lives were consumed with maintaining safety and sustenance, creating shelter and collecting rain.

Sid described for her the various texts he'd read about the culture and the theories concerning their disappearance. She stopped listening immediately and let her eyes run away, across the grass, along the ridges, pausing to follow a hawk's circling until it disappeared behind the sphere of a bush. Here they were about to turn away from the most inexplicably profound experience of the past year, and instead of celebrating the experience with her, he was doing what he did best—overwhelming the present with the burden of useless talk.

During the car ride back to the hotel, Sophie sat with the absurdity of Sid's idea that they might someday lose the memory of the ruins. For years, he had watched her addiction with some distance, wanting her to be healthy but not wanting to let go of the parts that served his own desire: her tendency to say yes to almost anything or the free pass that her mistakes provided when he spent too much money and refused to explain what he'd been up to. Had he never noticed how hard it was to not be consumed with thirst, with endless wanting? Had it crept past him that she had brushed against a lasting peace?

In the end, she found herself swallowed by the idea that she could ever forget that place, that it might be reduced to some neglected impression. The wild abandon of being naked under the open sky with him inside her, thoughtless, consumed with nothing but the silence of the desert and the hard won privilege of needing nothing more.

They slept for an hour before dinner. As usual, Sophie was the first one awake. The bar outside the door to their room was open. Smokers were scattered across the balcony, drinks in hand. A scraggly young man served her a club soda with lime—free of charge if she gave him a smile—and she found a chair around the corner with a view she hadn't seen. For a weekday, the streets below were heavy with traffic and the sidewalks packed with tourists and college students on the hunt for places to blow off steam.

Whenever her eyes landed on someone interesting, she tracked their progress, inventing narratives:

To an older man with a prophet's beard wearing two jackets and beanie over a baseball cap, she attributed a secret history of clandestine government work that had finally driven him mad.

Three college girls in Kappa Delta sweatshirts were traipsing through thrift stores for outfits that would impress the rest of their sisters. They were looking for the sort of party that would likely never be found in a mountain town—blacklights and strobes and citified beats pulsing hard enough to jiggle a concrete warehouse floor. She pictured them stepping into phone booths as wholesome, misplaced Midwesterners and emerging as caped and hooded neon heroes.

For a young couple wearing Grand Canyon T-shirts and speaking German, this was the honeymoon their parents had promised them, abroad in America with only each other and a lifetime of travel ahead. Her attempt at the accent was laughable, replacing w's with v's and so on, but it made Sophie laugh out loud to imagine that when the young woman pushed her mouth against her partner's ear she was telling him "How lucky vee are to be vandering here in a beautiful vorld of vonder."

The bartender swept past, emptying ashtrays and checking drinks. He paused beside her. "Everything okay, ma'am?"

Sophie hadn't realized that she was crying. She dragged her sleeve past her eyes and nodded.

"Let me know if you need something with a little more punch." He handed her a small stack of napkins. "We've got a beautiful new vodka from Colorado that I'd recommend."

"Isn't every vodka beautiful in its own way?" She pulled her sweater up over the lower half of her face to guard against the visceral chill of the breeze coming down from the mountains. "I'm okay for now, thank you."

"I could fix you a toddy if you're cold."

She asked him if he had hot tea, and he directed her to the place across the street.

The sign in the window declaring that the teashop was in fact a lounge was on point. It was appropriately dim with low Japanese style tables along one side of the room, square cushions for sitting, and a polished bar that would be at home in the best of British pubs. Sophie ordered a pot of black tea with an unpronounceable name and picked out a deck of playing cards from a selection of games. Other than a pair of young men on a first date at the table behind her and an older, professor-looking man reading at the end of the bar, she had the place to herself. The music was lounge-y as well—a curated list of songs from the Middle East across Asia and on to Latin America—predictable and yet, given the setting, not without its appeal. She shuffled the deck and set up a game of solitaire.

Her hands went through the motions of playing. Draw three, flip one, make a play, repeat. A sitar droned from a nearby speaker. Crows collected on the sidewalk outside her window to battle for a scrap of muffin that had been left behind. Their fussing drew her full attention, and when she turned to watch them, she saw Sid leaving the hotel. He zipped up his light jacket and turned left up the street without looking in her direction.

Sophie watched him, cheek pressed against the glass, until he was out of sight. A circle of window fog had formed in the shape of her profile around her head. She drew a pair of horns with her finger before returning to her game. One of the men made no secret of watching. He caught Sophie's eye and winked. His date turned to see what the fuss was about, and for several minutes the men took turns fogging their own window to make crude, cartoon-y portraits of each other, laughing and trading polite insults until they left the building hand in hand.

Sophie was proud to have inspired such a moment but jealous of its newness, the ridiculous, untamed excitement that comes with recently discovered attraction.

Still, she told herself, you had a small part in that. When they get married, you're a part of the story they'll tell about the night they got together. "There was this crazy lady that kept looking out the window at something. She was all by herself with a long face and a deck of cards. If it wasn't for her, I might never have invited Francis home."

A barista asked if she needed hot water and scooted away on her heels. Sophie switched to a different game with fewer rules. The cards were arranged in a pyramid to be matched in pairs that equaled unlucky thirteen.

When the barista returned, she watched Sophie play though a hand. "My grandmother plays that. She's eighty-five."

"My grandmother is dead," Sophie said, with as little emotion as possible. She made the last match and shuffled the deck. "But when she was still alive, she had no hands so I had to play for her."

The woman didn't check on her again.

She didn't know why she let the poor girl have it like that, but the longer she thought about it, the more she was sure she'd had a reason. Ms. A would know. Sophie took out her phone to call, then didn't. Talking to her sponsor—her analysis and preemptive advice—would bring an end to the internalized silence that she'd brought with her from ruins. Her eyes grew heavy, but not with sleep. The playlist was changed to jazz. An airy composition, light on structure, heavy on the trumpet. Miles Davis? Maybe? His later period. Less blue.

Sid reappeared some time later, a plastic grocery sack in one hand and large paper shopping bag in the other. Sophie chugged the last gulp of cold tea and followed him to the hotel parking lot, watching from behind a corner as he repacked the back of the car. If left on his own in an unfamiliar location, he was prone to heavy spending. There'd been times, vacations past, when he'd returned home with twice the gear he'd left with and new lines of credit from stores that had no Houston location. From the shopping bag, he produced a pair of binoculars, a sturdy-looking—and therefore expensive—pair of pants, a long-bladed knife, and what looked like a box of shells for the pistol. The pants went back in the bag. The rest he packed away.

Sophie pushed the heel of her hand to her face to keep from screaming when he pulled a handle of good bourbon and several small bottles of clear liquor from the other bag. He cracked the seal on one of them, took down a third of it in a gulp, and stuffed it in his jacket pocket. In less than a minute, he'd buried the rest of the bottles in their sleeping bags.

She stepped into view when the hatch slammed shut. Sid froze. They stood looking at each other, hands at their sides, like gunfighters ahead of a showdown.

"That's a lot of liquor, sir."

"You drank every drop of what I brought from home."

"How long would you have lasted if I hadn't?"

He came to stand beside her, gripped her shoulders. "I don't really pay attention the way you do."

Back in the room, Sophie scanned the national news and social media while he ripped the tags from the new pants and collected his things for a shower. More eclipse pictures. More idiotic presidential tweets.

Ms. A had posted a new status, asking for "prayers for a dear friend who's on her own in a dangerous situation." Program people responded appropriately, using coded sympathy to express their concern without revealing specific truths only they would understand. The non-addicts assumed that someone was in genuine jeopardy, an abusive marriage or a cancer diagnosis, maybe a victim of a violent crime. She thumbed through the feed until she was sure Sid was undressed, and as soon as she heard him humming the opening riff of "Smoke on the Water," his favorite shower song, she snatched up the keys and trotted back downstairs.

Including the handle, there were four bottles hidden in his sleeping bag and three in hers. That meant two more than they'd left home with. Whenever he shopped for booze, it was like he was anticipating a second Prohibition.

One by one, she opened each bottle. The smell of it took her breath as a tiny river of liquor flowed to the curb, collecting leaves and bits of litter along the way. It became a torrent when she chased the vodka with the whiskey.

She let out a low whistle. "Maker's 46. Nothing but the good shit for Sid."

Sophie patted at the droplets on the cuffs of her jeans, buried the last of her anger beneath a welcome wave of power, and went back upstairs to wait for her turn at the shower.

For the rest of the evening, they sat on the balcony, sipping sodas and snacking on appetizers. A female bartender had taken over the upstairs bar. Sid tipped the woman like they'd been drinking fancy cocktails, and in exchange she gave them bottomless fries. He dipped a potato in something called aioli and fed it to Sophie, who bit his finger with gentle teeth and moved closer.

"So you're not upset with me?" Sid's skin was sunkissed with a blush of rosy emotion underneath. He seemed almost proud, magnanimous and incredulous at the same time. "I thought for sure you were going to skin me back there at the car."

"For which part?"

He lit one of her cigarettes and kept it for himself. "You name it."

"You almost sound disappointed that I didn't."

When he looked at her, suddenly, like it was a surprise she was still sitting there, his eyes contained that softness that always broke through her dissatisfaction. They were brighter, bluer, not unlike the desert sky that had caused them both to swoon. Once, she would have believed she was catching him in the act of loving her, and on their better days, days like today, that still held true. Still, the skeptic inside her refused to stay silent.

"I don't know what it is that I should say. What you want to hear." He stood like a boy in trouble, his movements shifty, waiting for punishment. "What will make this go away."

Sophie pulled him to her, opened her mouth to receive the smoke he exhaled, and leaned all the way in. The crowd of drinkers around them appeared oblivious, but she imagined that anyone watching might have assumed they were on a first date. The couple from the teashop passed through her mind, and their energy, taut with newness, seemed as foreign as the feelings she was attempting to resurrect.

She pulled away. "Your spit is boozy."

"That okay?"

"Just finish the damn bottle before I take it from you. But don't brush your teeth."

The chill of the outside air had stolen into their room. Sid closed the bathroom door to freshen up. Sophie undressed and ran her hands across the gooseflesh that covered her arms, her chest, and every other place she had hair. He came to her, beads of water and liquor clinging to the stubble of his chin. Once the lights were out, they lay entwined, unmoving, listening as the party raged on just outside their door. Soon he was sleeping. She wished they were still lying in the ruins with a bed of weathered stone grating at their backs, counting stars until they reached infinity. Sophie's heartbeat was a pulsar in her throat and, vibrating faintly beneath it, was the premonition that they'd never be so close again.

No Gas in Chloride

Somehow, they were both awake at daylight, packed and out of the room ahead of schedule. A quick stop for coffee at a vegetarian place he'd read about turned into a full meal of huevos rancheros and oat muffins, with travel mugs, T-shirts, and five pounds of coffee beans—roasted in-house at eighteen bucks a pop—to carry home. Sophie wanted to ask him how much money he had left, how long before he admitted he'd spent too much and asked her for her credit card, but the mood inside the car was still light so she shoved the question into a back corner and watched the pines outside her window blur together in an endless swath of green.

She had no idea where they were headed next, only that it was in the high desert somewhere near Las Vegas, as far west as he'd planned to travel this time out. Ms. A had pressed her to find out, but every time she asked him, Sid seemed intent on keeping it a surprise. "You're gonna love it," he'd say with more pride than confidence and follow it up with some version of "It'll be way cooler than that time we camped Enchanted Rock."

Ms. A was forever a skeptic. "What's stopping him from pushing into Nevada?"

No matter how she answered, Sophie would find herself pinned between her sponsor's need to question every decision and her boyfriend's thoughtless determination. "I'll just walk off into the desert and hide behind a boulder until he backs off."

"Don't step on a rattlesnake." Ms. A had said through a forced cackle. "I'd imagine there's more rocks than people where you're headed."

They couldn't settle on a playlist. Sid was feeling feisty and wanted to sing. Sophie's thoughts were still in Flagstaff where the late morning light would have rendered every angle and curve of the city into abstractions of color and shade. No matter how hard he pressed her, she couldn't imagine a soundtrack that would fit her mood.

"Just pick something," she told him. "Whatever it is, I can take it."

Instead of just making a decision, he chose to debate his choices aloud. Slipknot versus Harry Belafonte. Billy Joel or Elton John. Ten seconds into each track, he'd change his mind and play another. Nearly half an hour had passed before Sophie snatched the iPod, hit shuffle, and stuffed it under her seat. Sid pouted all the way to Kingman, Arizona, where a sign for an IN-N-OUT made him cut across three lanes to the exit, bouncing in his seat like a kid trying not to pee.

"When I pulled a move like that back in Texas, you tore me a new one for trying to get you killed."

Sid laughed. "That's because you weren't focused on the road ahead. You were all looking off to the side, trying to see what they were up to over in Mexico." He slid into a parking place and pointed at a man double-fisting a burger and fries. "You can't expect me to waste time driving around when that's the prize that awaits."

She asked him to bring her a strawberry milkshake and waited till he was inside to turn on her phone. Two missed calls. Two voicemails from Ms. A, the first left just before midnight, the second just after:

"I guess you're asleep or your phone's turned off or dead or you're somewhere where there's no signal. I don't know why we didn't talk about this before you left—I reckon I'm a bad sponsor—but I've been thinking that you should seriously consider catching a meeting while you're in a city. I did some digging. You've got a couple of options there in Flagstaff. One at eight A.M. One at ten. Both walking distance from your hotel." Her voice broke, and after a long pause the remaining words were drained of strength. *"Sophie . . . I'm . . . I can't accept that I'm the only one who's worried here."*

Sophie hung up before the second message played. When she shifted to get comfortable, a white pain lit up between her shoulder blades and above her left hip. It was a specific tension that came when there were hard choices to make or consequences that could not be avoided. Standing before the judge to receive her sentence and giving up the routine of working every day at the bar. The decision to stop drinking and to stay unemployed until the right opportunity came along. Her mouth was so flooded with want that she had to swallow twice to get it all down.

Was it finally time to sell? Had her father been gone long enough? Would he return in dreams to ask her about business as he had in the months that followed his passing? She could see him at the kitchen table in his long sleeves and slicked back hair. In front of him were coffee and cigarettes and more regrets than satisfaction.

The Hawthorne hadn't aged well, and neither had the crowd of rednecks and country dancers that had made it a success. They'd been replaced by youngsters in tight, dark jeans with haircuts that cost the same as a week of groceries. Sophie had never heard of craft beer until they started showing up, looking for a bit of authenticity to co-opt. She had allowed Sid to keep the place running for her, and in that time she had come to see him as the one employee she could never fire.

Someone tapped on the window. An adolescent mother, on the road, newly homeless, looking for enough money to feed her toddler and find a bed to pass the night. Sophie gave her what change she had and sent her into the restaurant. She texted Sid to buy them lunch and a gift card for another meal. He wasn't one for charity, but he wouldn't know how to say no either.

Ms. A's second message was fraught with warning. *"When you get back, we have to talk. I . . . don't think I can do this with you anymore, Sophie. I had to call my sponsor this afternoon to keep from blowing fifteen years."*

The one-year medallion was buried at the bottom of her bag. Sophie turned it over and over, tracing the "I" with her thumbnail. She held it to her lips the way she'd seen others do in meetings, as if kissing tarnished bronze would transform temptation into resolution, turn a hard choice into an afterthought. The metal warmed against her mouth, its taste like water drawn from a copper pipe.

She began the Serenity Prayer, stopping halfway through at the word "courage."

She began the mantra she'd used in the earliest weeks of recovery: "I will not drink," repeated until the thirst was gone.

She began to wonder if there would ever be another place as quiet as the ruins of Northern Arizona, where no thought dared to challenge the whisper of the endless wind.

"I don't need a fucking drink, though," she said out loud. "I don't even want one."

But the endlessness of staying sober was even less appealing. It had become to her a condition that existed simply to perpetuate itself. The thing she did to stay out of trouble, to keep everyone around her happy— excluding Sid—until it had gone on for so long she'd forget what her life was like before. Finding a new sponsor, just the thought of it, seemed unbearable. She'd have to leave the Tuesday meeting to avoid the weekly embarrassment.

Whatever was supposed to happen, she wasn't going to figure it out right then. Her blood called for nicotine. She stashed the chip in the fifth pocket of her jeans and rolled her window. A second later, Sid's hand reached through it with her milkshake and a bonus gift of fries.

"Holy dogshit, that was spectacular." He looked happier than he did after he'd just had an orgasm. "I ordered off the secret menu. 3x3. Animal style. Almost got you one, too, so I could eat your leftovers."

"I don't think that's much of a secret. Even I heard of it." The milkshake tasted good, but she could picture it being better with a slug of rum. "Did you get my text?"

He climbed in and pointed past her to where the homeless girl and her child were sitting at an outside table with a full tray between them. "They wouldn't let me pay for her food, so I gave her a twenty."

Tears were running down her face before she noticed them. This business of crying without knowing it was becoming a problem. When Sid asked her what was wrong, she could only shake her head. When he asked if he'd done good, she couldn't do more than nod.

It wasn't until they'd turned off the interstate and gone a good ways out of town that he realized they needed gas. The highway traversed the lip of a bowl-shaped, brushy valley. Mountains ran parallel on either side. Scattered near their feet were a handful of prefabricated buildings and the occasional windmill, the only marks of humanity in an otherwise empty land. Billboards advertising upcoming concerts by washed up rock stars at a casino in Laughlin, Nevada. A small brown and white cow, legs stiff with rigor mortis, lay forgotten in the shimmering heat just beyond a sign indicating that there was a town hidden somewhere up ahead.

Questions bloomed and withered. She leaned over to check the gas gauge. "So this isn't where we're camping?"

"Who the hell would want to camp in a place called Chloride? Sounds toxic." He tugged a water bottle from under his seat, took a swig, and coughed hard enough for Sophie to know it wasn't H_2O. "Now that I think about it, though, out here there probably isn't a whole hell of a lot that isn't."

"Maybe it's a ghost town."

A second sip. A softer cough. "Maybe it's where people go to die."

"Maybe that cow back there was its last surviving resident. Maybe she decided it was time to find a better place to live." When Sophie pressed her hand against it, the window was hot to the touch. "I feel like we should cover her with something."

"The world was mooooo-ving, she was right there with it, and she was," Sid sang, laughing so hard at himself the car nearly left the road. He leaned in toward Sophie. "Hey, hey!"

"Is this the day you finally kill me trying to be clever?"

This good mood of his was noxious, nearly unnerving, but she didn't want to be a buzzkill so she bit down on the insides of her cheeks.

After the first mile, the road into Chloride turned to pressed limestone like micro-speedbumps, and the car stuttered rigidly across them. She folded her arms across her chest to control the bouncing and ignored his offer to "help her out with those."

The best way to change the subject was to question his attention to detail. "I hope the spare tire's in good shape. Did you check the shocks before we left?"

"Car's brand new, Sophie. Forty-seven miles when I drove it off the lot."

"What if they forgot to inspect it? What if they took you for a sucker and let you take off without checking things out?"

This was just the sort of fight that Sid was built for. Over the years, he'd perfected these elaborately detailed, nearly breathless sermons that explained exactly how wrong she was and why. With this trip, so far, they'd managed to avoid getting into it with each other, but Sophie found herself craving old routines. Satisfied, she propped her feet on the dash to annoy him further, lit a cigarette, and tuned him out. It took him two more miles to figure out she wasn't listening. She was almost disappointed when he let it drop.

The land around them hadn't changed, but there were signs that civilization had come and gone again. Sun-blasted Winnebagos with solar panels and broken windows. Empty doghouses and barbed wire squares that might have held livestock once upon a time. Abandoned boats and automobiles and scrapyards with stacks of rusted metal parts. Four out of five homes rested on flat tires, like plans for a mass exodus had been derailed by saboteurs.

Up ahead, a dark figure appeared, walking down the center of the road as if it were a footpath, seemingly oblivious that they were drawing near. Sid tapped the horn in patterns of three until the man moved to the right just enough to let them by. He was outfitted head to toe in leather motorcycle gear with something propped against his shoulder. At a distance, it was impossible to see what it was through all the dust in the air.

"Check that shit out, would you?" Sid pulled as far as he could to the left and tapped the dashboard beside the outdoor thermometer display.

"It's one-oh-six out there, and old Mad Max is dressed like he's about to push his hog through a Minnesota winter."

"They say you get used to the heat."

He snorted. "That's like saying you'll grow gills if you spend most of your time in the water."

They were less than a hundred yards away when the man turned to face them.

Sophie's heart rate tripled. "That's a rifle. He's carrying a fucking rifle, Sid."

He leaned forward with a gasp and slowed to a crawl. "That's a fucking AR-15. And you thought that good old Las Cruces was apocalyptic."

Several seconds of garbled conversation followed with no clear inclination as to how they might proceed. The man raised a gloved hand to wave them down, and when the car was at a stop, he stood outside Sophie's window until he figured out she wasn't going to open it for him.

"Damn it, Sophie." Sid waved him over. "Sir, you need a ride or something?"

His voice was a lovely baritone, rich and deep with prominent Northeastern vowels. "Am I safe in assuming that you two have lost your way?"

The man put his back against the car, weapon cradled in his arms. Black, bloodthirsty, and malignant, it called to mind the surge of mass shootings that had dominated the news for months. She hoped he couldn't see what she could, that Sid's hands were shaking in his lap. When it became clear that he couldn't find an answer, she leaned past him. "Can you tell us where to find the nearest gas station?"

"You're not about to run out, are you?" The man smiled at her, revealing a row of immaculately whitened teeth. "You won't find no gas in Chloride. Not unless you can get ahold of somebody willing to siphon off a half gallon. Probably cost you ten bucks or more but if you're in a pinch."

Sid discovered his courage. "We've got a little better than twenty miles yet."

"That's enough to get you over to Dolan. Built a nice new filling station right off the highway about a quarter mile." He noticed Sid's eyes were on the rifle. "You want to give my lovely Betty a hug, don't you?"

Watching the men pass the gun between them like a pair of kids at show and tell was too much crazy for Sophie to wrap her head around. There weren't many Texans that hadn't spent time with a father or an uncle or a cousin at a firing range, but seeing the potential for ultimate chaos in her boyfriend's hands laid the last of her respect for him to rest. He was too eager, jaw clenched, top lip cocked in a snarl, pointing the muzzle at distant windshields and fence posts before lifting it skyward to track a buzzard hovering high above them on the wind. The stranger said something to him in a low tone and when the gun went off, she screamed.

"That bird's a damn big target," Sid said, surrendering the rifle to its keeper. "But I'm kind of glad I missed it."

They bumped along the road back to the highway and turned north. Sid swallowed compulsively like he did when he could feel her disappointment. "That was fucking surreal, wasn't it?"

"I don't think I've got a name for what that was."

"What was I supposed to do? A man with a gun flags you down—especially a gun that could blow the engine if he hit it just right—when he offers to let you take a shot, you take the shot."

She reclined her seat back all the way. "Why does he call it Betty?"

"You won't believe it," he said, fiddling with the music. "He watches *Mad Men.*"

A church organ playing random notes overtook the roar of their tires on the highway, increasing in volume until it filled the car. It sounded like a funeral. For several seconds, she couldn't place the song until a guitar faded in. A happy jangle of chords. When the bass and drums joined the mix, Sophie recognized the torture she was about to endure.

"You're joking. U-fucking-2?"

"I was going to play it earlier, but you were crying."

"I'm about to start crying again."

He was playing along one-handed air guitar, strumming his thumbnail across the side seam of his cargo pants. "Just go with it. Once we get there, it will all make sense."

"How far away is 'there?'"

"The next exit. Same town as the gas station." He squeezed her hand, her wrist, her shoulder, then patted her on the head. "We're about to fulfill a dream, Sophie." And then he was singing along with the next track, half a beat behind the melody, oblivious of pitch with a quarter of the range.

The car felt tight, too full of dissonance to even sit comfortably. Sophie put her head out the window, but the rush of hot wind was no match for the sanctimonious racket. A grasshopper collided with her forehead and popped. She pulled one of Sid's white undershirts from the back seat to wipe away the guts and tossed it to the side of the road. In the passenger side mirror, it twisted briefly in their slipstream before surrendering to the ground.

What We Came Here to Find

The Chevron station was the nicest building in Dolan Springs. Every other structure looked like it had been made with materials collected during a scavenger hunt. Sophie stared out the window at the dried out nothing around her, refusing to accept that they were near the end of the line they'd been traveling. Sid was in commando mode, on task, focused on the directions he'd stashed in the glove box. U2 was still playing, but faintly.

Their ultimate destination was still a secret, but he guaranteed they'd be there soon. "It's gonna be magic, Soph. Serious mystical shit. By the time we wake up tomorrow, you won't want to go back to Texas."

Negotiating heavy traffic was an unexpected delight. The road was packed with tourist shuttles and single families in dusty SUVs. It stretched out before them in a straight line past the horizon.

Sid's voice usually jumped an octave whenever he was feeling claustrophobic. Pinned between a minibus and a local driver pulling a banged up truck in tow, he was nearing a falsetto.

"This is basically the back door to the Grand Canyon. The West Rim. Lake Mead." His fingers drummed against the wheel. "But no one knows the place we're going. For the next three days, it's just you and me."

Digging through her purse to find her chip, she asked him, "What the hell's wrong with the front door?"

The answer was lengthy, complicated, and incomplete. More vague references to magic and hints at nostalgia, like he genuinely believed she was on board with this mystery.

They passed the town's lone restaurant, which was across the street from its only grocery. There was zero probability she'd find a meeting here if she needed one. Drinking would be key to one's survival, as necessary as food, even oxygen. If she were living in this wasteland, her monthly booze budget would be higher than the rent.

She was ready for the big reveal, an end to the ridiculous suspense. Whatever it was, she wouldn't react the way he wanted. She never did, but he never stopped trying.

The only thing she knew for certain was that they'd be camping. Looking at the abundance of hard, flat ground, punctuated with small boulders and tall spiky plants that reminded her of the trees from the Lorax movie, she could see that a comfortable night of sleep wasn't part of the plan.

By the end of tomorrow, they'd be fighting. He'd go for a walk to get over it. She'd hide inside the tent with her cigarettes, sipping bottled water, fantasizing about the bottles of liquor in the back of the car.

As far as she knew, Sid hadn't shared their location with anyone. Sophie sat on a blanket while he lugged gear from the car, waiting for her phone to lock onto a signal so she could send their GPS coordinates to Ms. A. They were miles from the road, in a rocky clearing surrounded by an entire forest of Dr. Seuss trees. The sun was lower in the sky but still menacing. Huge black ants ran around her like confused pedestrians. Still searching for a signal, the phone's battery dipped below fifty percent.

"You don't have to just sit around, Soph." He held out her hiking shoes and pointed at a thin track that zigzagged away toward the mountains. "That's a game trail. If you follow it, you might see some antelope, maybe a coyote when it gets closer to dark." He handed her a fresh bottle of water and an aluminum pole with a spike at one end.

"I'm not planning on doing any skiing."

"It's so you don't bust your ass." His grin was genuine. "You can also use it for snakes and other creepy-crawlies."

"What do I do if I see one?"

"The sun's too hot for reptiles. Just don't kick over any rocks or step in any holes. Make sure you investigate the ground before you sit."

"What if I get lost?"

"Stick to the path, and you'll be all right. But if not," he said, then cupped his hands around his mouth and shouted. The sound rolled across the desert to the foot of the mountains and back. "Do that every couple of minutes till I find you."

If someone were to ask her why she went along with the idea of walking through this landscape alone, she would only be able to say that initially she wanted to put a little distance between them so she could freak the fuck out in private. He was never more irritating than when he was trying to calm her down. But the further from camp she got, the lighter her insides felt. She thought about the trips they'd taken together, closer to home, when he tried to show her outdoor stuff. She wished she'd paid more attention. The same could be said of how they went about everyday living. Sophie didn't want to need him.

There were faint footprints in the sand—some with hooves and some with toes—that made the trail easier to follow. The wind wasn't as full-bodied as it had been outside of Flagstaff and if it had a voice it was too faint for her to hear. This didn't keep her from stopping in the shadow of one of the crazy tree-plants, eyes closed, ears straining for a similar connection. The attempt alone was satisfying. She resumed walking, settled into a rhythm, and lost track of time.

Clouds began to gather, blocking enough of the sun for the temperature to drop noticeably. Thunder rumbled on the other side of the mountains. In between a pair of low hills, she found a large boulder a few feet from the path and, after a thorough inspection, took a seat. There were birds all around, but the only one she recognized was a reddish hawk perched in between the spikey leaves of a tree with its eyes on the ground, waiting for a meal to reveal itself.

Her phone chimed in her pocket with a text message. One bar of signal, enough for it to come through. But it was only a warning that she was near her monthly data limit. The battery had dropped to forty-one percent.

A wispy column of smoke rose above the treetops. Sid had built a fire and would have started dinner. She sent her coordinates to Ms. A and got ready to head back to camp.

At her feet was a single footprint, bigger than a man's fist, four round toes with a triangular pad beneath them, similar to the marks that stray cats left in the dirt on the hood of a car. A quick Internet search confirmed that there was a mountain lion in the vicinity. Even if Sid had been there to remind her that most predators loved the chase, he could never have convinced her that it was a bad idea to run.

She burst into camp and went straight for the water. He was sitting on his heels beside the fire with a plate of roasted sausages in his lap. After changing into thick leggings and a sweatshirt, Sophie found her cigarettes and lighter and an empty can for an ashtray waiting for her on a table dressed with a checkered cloth and purple wildflowers. When the food was ready, sliced links with skillet potatoes, they ate in silence.

If he noticed that she was still shaking, he ignored it. She couldn't help but notice that when he wasn't chewing his jaw was clenched.

At twilight, he lit fancy candle lanterns and brought Navajo blankets from the tent. The last of the clouds had dissipated, exposing the bulk of the Milky Way stretching toward them from the south. It was cool enough for jackets. Sid tossed piñon logs on top of the oak he used for cooking. They smelled like incense, which made her feel a little bit at home.

They started small-talking about plans for tomorrow and the rest of the trip. Should we take it easy the first day? Eggs and toast for breakfast, pork loin with carrots, canned beans, and onion for lunch and dinner? Should we hike the foothills or cut straight across the forest to the edge of town and back? He was already trying to convince her they should stay an extra day.

"Can you tell me what we came here to find?"

His eyes rolled skyward. "I was convinced you'd already figured it out and just didn't give a fuck."

"You made such a big deal about this magic secret you've been keeping, I thought we'd be going through some portal to visit aliens or wearing pointy hats and chanting spells."

"Holy shit. Joshua trees." His face brightened briefly, and he walked to the edge of the firelight to grip a low hanging branch. "I thought the U2 was a dead giveaway."

This is why we drove hallway across the country, she said to herself. "You're serious," she said aloud.

"When I was a kid, it was my favorite album. You can't tell me you didn't have a copy."

The best response was not to give an answer. If she did, the debate would rage till dawn.

He pulled his chair closer to her. "Don't tell nobody. I got to protect my reputation."

The dark was rich with sound. Night birds peeping. The yip of coyotes in a squabble. Somewhere in the distance was a herd of cattle, groaning.

Sophie could feel his attention squeezing like a tourniquet around the issue he'd been sitting on, hyper-focused, watchful. This was how it happened. He'd take his time, arrange the words in tight formation so she couldn't find a loophole, pick his moment, and strike.

It was in her best interest to speak first. "You didn't tell me about the mountain lions."

"I didn't know there were any here." His eyes caught a glint of fire. "I wondered why you were running cross country, but I wasn't sure if I should ask."

She jumped slightly at a rustle in the brush behind her. With all the research he'd done, all the planning, he'd somehow missed that there were animals big enough to eat them.

"You should always ask, Sid."

She realized the moment she'd handed him, lit a cigarette, and turned her chair to face him.

"Then let me ask this." The darkness made it difficult to tell if he was actually angry or simply curious. "Why'd you pour out all the liquor?"

It took her a few seconds to remember she had done it. Flagstaff seemed so far away, so long ago. "Why do you insist on keeping it around?"

Without another word, he stood and walked out into the night. His boots crunched in a wide circle around the camp. This was a show of righteous anger, one that was undercut by the obvious fear of straying too far.

Sophie couldn't remember a time when she'd forced him into silence. If she ever had, she was sure it would've taken much longer.

There's a little magic, for ya, she thought, and wished she had a shot to celebrate.

The only suitable place to pee was a few yards past the tent. Holding a small flashlight between her teeth, she squatted between two trees and let it go. There was a scraping sound away to the left, like a heavy weight dragging through coarse gravel, too far away to shine a light on, too close to let her bladder empty all the way. She stood, bounced twice to shake off any moisture, and hurried back to the fire.

Fresh off his tantrum, Sid was sitting at the table, rubbing a white cloth along a short length of black metal. He was polishing the barrel of the pistol. Two boxes of shells were close at hand. Suddenly, Sophie wasn't sure she wanted to sit down.

"Thought I might put a few rounds into one of these trees." With one eye closed, he sighted down the barrel. "I was going to wait until tomorrow, but shooting always puts me in a better mood."

"I'd completely forgotten you brought it."

"There's a better reason I should do it now." He waved the muzzle around them. "While I was walking, I heard something moving through the brush—probably your mountain lion—hanging around until we go to sleep."

"I heard it, too."

"They say you won't know it when the big cats are coming. Maybe this one's gotten lazy." With a flourish, he inserted the clip and chambered a round. "Time to make a little noise. Scare that fucker off."

The Sid she was looking at now felt different than the one who'd tried to shoot down a buzzard back in Chloride. She didn't like him any better, but he at least seemed a bit more confident.

"Cover your ears, Soph." He lifted the gun toward the stars and fired.

Birds exploded from the trees around them as the shot echoed back from the mountains. A small animal, rabbit-sized, ran past the campfire and disappeared. Sid shot the trunks of the three nearest trees.

He flipped the butt of the gun to Sophie. "Want to give it a try?"

The grip was warm, the barrel too hot to touch.

"What should I shoot at?"

"Anything you want. Just keep the business end aimed away from me and the car."

She couldn't believe how hard it was to pull the trigger until she'd done it. She was equally surprised to be eager to do it again. With her first shot, she aimed for the North Star. The second round she sent toward Mars.

Sid looked like a proud father. "Empty the clip."

Except for the three points of light that made Orion's belt, the rest of the stars were chosen for their brightness. The last squeeze was a dry fire. She asked if they could do it again.

They sat together at the table so that he could teach her how to reload, holding one box of shells back in case of emergency. The empty casings were tossed into the glowing coals.

Just as Sid was about to take a second turn, a volley of gunfire erupted in the distance. They both jumped. Three more shots rang out in rapid sequence, and when they faded, even the wind had gone still.

It felt like a warning. Someone was out there—closer than either of them had suspected—with strong opinions about who should be doing the shooting. Almost immediately, he went from being startled to being pissed. "Which direction was that coming from? Could you tell?"

She couldn't if she'd wanted to. "I think we should maybe go."

"Driving back here was hard enough in the daytime. We're stuck here, so let's figure something out."

Without preparing her ahead of time, he fired twice and waited for them to respond. Thirty seconds passed. He fired two more and cursed the distant shooter for failing to reply.

Sophie took the gun from him and topped off the clip. She had an intuition about what might convince the person to respond. "I'm gonna try something. Be ready to hand me that other clip."

She fired once and counted five. Fired twice, counted again, and fired three more. The pattern was repeated perfectly.

He snatched the gun from her and changed the sequence. The other shooter held off.

"What a waste of ammunition," Sid pouted, and chewed his bottom lip.

Sophie took it back and fired six shots in the original order. Her new friend returned fire and they went back and forth in various combinations, like building sentences from percussive waves of sound. The reciprocity was exhilarating. It reminded her of a drinking game or taking shots of whiskey with the stranger on the next barstool.

She wasn't sorry over how much she was enjoying the attention. "I can't help if they like me more than they like you."

"Phone's don't work for shit out here. Maybe this is how they communicate. Like, 'Hey there, Billy Bob, I'm cooking up some meth if you want to stop by later.'" His humor was at its best whenever his feelings were hurt. "If we were in Switzerland, we'd be yodeling."

Inside the tent, the air was thicker. It still held a bit of heat. They lay beside each other, not touching, fully dressed with their boots on in case they had to move.

She couldn't see it when Sid propped himself on his elbow.

"Why did you decide to drink in Las Cruces?"

"We're going to do this, aren't we?" She felt around for her cigarettes and lit one. "If you want to have this conversation, don't complain about the smoke."

He unzipped the windows for ventilation. "Why didn't you just drink with me at the bar?"

"I tell you this every time we talk about it. You don't plan to screw up like that. You just keep resisting it until you just can't do it anymore." She cleared her throat several times until the knot that had formed there was manageable. "My sponsor has been hinting for months that I should leave you."

He sighed. "Smart lady."

"I agree. But why do you think so?"

"Because I've been on pins and needles waiting for you to fail."

This confession wasn't surprising. It didn't hurt her to hear it. In fact, it didn't trouble her at all. Sophie sat up. "Is that why you keep bringing so much home?"

"I like you better when you're drinking. Since you quit, it's like we've lost our glue."

If she were to admit that she agreed with him about the distance, she'd have to confess that she never saw alcohol as a lubricant to maintain harmony. Never thought of it as the tie that binds. Liquor equaled freedom. It never held her accountable or asked that she be mindful of her own suffering. She was powerless over alcohol, but the power that it gave her was more than worth the cost. Without it, she was simply existing.

"I don't want to deal with this right now." She laid on her side with her back to him. "Just go to sleep. Please."

Sid talked to himself by pretending to talk to her for several minutes, answering his own questions with a high-pitched imitation of her voice. Finally, he took her silence to heart and stopped needling.

Sophie fought to keep control of her thoughts. She had made a decision, but she wasn't sure what it was until she heard him settle into sleep.

Unzipping the tent door was the hardest part. If she woke him, the questions would start all over again. The car keys were tucked into a corner beside the pistol. She pushed the unlock button and stepped outside.

Her phone was dead, but a rosy glow above the eastern horizon gave her an idea of the time. With the flashlight, she found her bag and a bottle of water, and wrote him a note on a napkin: *Gone hiking. Be back soon.*

As she made her way through the Joshua trees to the dry wash, she was worried he'd wake up to hear her feet crunching away from him. Other than that, leaving was the easiest thing in the world.

With a little luck, he'd sleep for a few hours, giving her time to get to Dolan Springs before he figured out the truth and came looking. She'd go to the grocery store when it opened and ask if she could charge her phone. When it was working, she'd text Ms. A: *I'm not coming back to Texas. You can find someone else to make you want to drink.*

She imagined her father's gaunt, ghostly figure stepping from the shadows with both hands up, pleading silently for her to reconsider. "What will happen to my life's work?" she heard him murmur. Not, "What will happen to my baby girl when she's out there all alone?"

These are the reasons why a person stays, Papa, she wanted to tell him. They stay because it requires nothing of them. Because there's no change that isn't forced upon them. They stay for court orders and family businesses for which they aren't built to maintain. They stay because the one they thought they cared for still resembles, however faintly, the person they believed they fell for but simply fell into. Because that person will always be there to keep them connected to that which they needed to leave but couldn't. Eventually, they get tired of playing possum when a life gets scary and keeping secrets when it's finally safe.

Stepping around him, out of reach of grasping hands, Sophie flicked the light on and quickly off again to establish bearings. The road was still in front of her. The night had fallen silent at her passing, and into this sudden vacuum went the last of her hesitation.

"I can't tell you why—" she whispered, to her father, to Ms. A, and to Sid, presuming he might shut up long enough to listen. "Why isn't really a why, is it? It's just a word we repeat, a way of begging for meaning until better questions find their way into the light."

She stepped cautiously across limestone gravel, which was now illuminated by the risen moon. She looked up, past its full face and through the star field beyond in the direction some believed they'd discover heaven. "I require a different darkness now. I don't know what that looks like, but I know there's no room inside it for anyone else."

Sophie passed through the Dr. Seuss trees and onto paved highway. She'd find out what the options were for getting out of town, show a little leg if she had to, try to charm a tour bus driver into letting her on board. Maybe he'd take her to the casino over in Laughlin where the rock stars go when they're no longer rock stars and can't find a better gig. It wasn't Las Vegas, but it seemed like a drinking town. She'd rent a room by the week, get a bar job, get into some trouble and some day, when she was ready, she'd find a meeting and tell the group her story, but all under a different name.

Acknowledgments

From the endless list of names of those I would like to thank for their guidance and support, I would like to begin with Greg Oaks, my first mentor and now my dear friend, for setting me on the path. Without you, there would be none of this.

Antonya Nelson, who showed me what it means to be an artist and made sure I didn't forget. Thank you for encouraging me to move ahead with this journey, for sending me into the desert.

Alexander Parsons, David MacLean, and Aaron Reynolds, who taught me what it means to be a working writer, the habits and practices of craft.

My writing mentors during my time at New Mexico State: Rus Bradburd, Evan Lavender-Smith, Lily Hoang, and the rest of my New Mexico State family, including Carmen Gimenez-Smith, Connie Voisine, Richard Greenfield, Elizabeth Schirmer, Tracey Miller-Tomlinson, Ryan Cull, Lydia Apodaca, and all my Las Cruces friends and peers. Your love and patient support carried me through. The lessons you shared—both in and outside the classroom—gave me a new shape.

My sister and brother in a most unholy trinity, Emily Alex and Brady Richards.

My chosen Houston family, especially Kathryn Tyler and Kyle Johnson, for teaching me the importance of community. My new San Antonio family, for understanding what that means.

My mother, Ann Stockwell, my siblings Bob, Gilda, Mark, Gale, their significant others and all their many descendants. Thanks for never giving up. Thanks for looking the other way. Thanks for keeping the light on so I can find my way home.

Kelly Stewart Porter, who had the patience to proofread this story in manuscript form.

To J. Bruce Fuller, Lisa Tremaine, and everyone at Texas Review Press: Thank you for making this little book a reality.

About the Author

Patrick Stockwell is an Inprint MD Anderson Foundation fellow at the University of Houston. He holds an MFA from New Mexico State University.